SCOOBY-DOO!™

Cuyahoga Falls
Library
Cuyahoga Falls, Ohio

HEAR NO EVIL

EARL KRESS, WRITER   JOHN DELANEY, PENCILLER
TERRY BEATTY, INKER   TOM ORZECHOWSKI, LETTERER
PAUL BECTON, COLORIST   DIGITAL CHAMELEON, SEPARATIONS
HARVEY RICHARDS, ASS'T EDITOR   JOAN HILTY, EDITOR

Spotlight

VISIT US AT
www.abdopublishing.com

Reinforced library bound edition published in 2010 by Spotlight, a division of the ABDO Group, 8000 West 78th Street, Edina, Minnesota 55439. Spotlight produces high-quality reinforced library bound editions for schools and libraries. Published by agreement with Warner Bros.—A Time Warner Company. All rights reserved. Used under authorization.

Printed in the United States of America, Melrose Park, Illinois.
092009
012010

 PRINTED ON RECYCLED PAPER

Library of Congress Cataloging-in-Publication Data

Kress, Earl.
  Scooby-doo in Hear no evil / writer, Earl Kress ; penciller, John Delaney ; inker, Terry Beatty ; colorist, Paul Becton ; letterer, Tom Orzechowski. -- Reinforced library bound ed.
      p. cm. -- (Scooby-Doo graphic novels)
  ISBN 978-1-59961-694-0
  1. Graphic novels. I. Delaney, John. II. Scooby-Doo (Television program) III. Title. IV. Title: Hear no evil.
  PZ7.7.K73Sc 2010
  741.5'973--dc22

                                        2009032899

All Spotlight books have reinforced library bindings and
are manufactured in the United States of America.

EARL KRESS, WRITER   JOHN DELANEY, PENCILLER
TERRY BEATTY, INKER   TOM ORZECHOWSKI, LETTERER
PAUL BECTON, COLORIST   DIGITAL CHAMELEON, SEPARATIONS
HARVEY RICHARDS, ASS'T EDITOR   JOAN HILTY, EDITOR

I TOLD LAURA DAD'S JUST *CRACKING UP!*

≶SIGH≷ THIS IS MY BROTHER LUKE. PLEASE EXCUSE HIM -- SOMETIMES HE CAN BE *SO* CRASS!

THEY SAY THE *CRASS* IS ALWAYS *CREENER* ON THE OTHER SIDE!

RHEE, HEE, HEE!

YES! THE *OTHER SIDE!* I BELIEVE THERE'S SOME-THING *PARANORMAL* GOING ON IN THIS HOUSE!

SO, THE FAMILY COMPANY IS CALLED *HUGHES INDUSTRIES.* WHAT DOES IT MANUFACTURE?

WE HAVE A LOT OF GOVERNMENT CONTRACTS FOR DIFFERENT PROJECTS.

BUT WE SPECIALIZE IN *ULTRA-MINIATURIZATION!*

THIS WRISTWATCH IS ACTUALLY A *DIGITAL CAMERA* CAPABLE OF PRODUCING A PHOTO WITH *7.1 MILLION PIXELS!*

MAYBE THEY COULD MINIATURIZE OUR *STOMACHS!* THEN WE WOULDN'T BE SO *HUNGRY* ALL THE TIME, EH, SCOOB?

RUNH-UH! RI RIKE RUNGER!

WELL, GOTTA RUN. NICE MEETING YOU ALL!

AND THIS IS A COMPUTER AS *POWERFUL* AS THE *FASTEST DESKTOP*, YET *BARELY* THE SIZE OF A *CREDIT CARD!*

JINKIES! THEY'LL HAVE TO *MINIATURIZE* YOUR *FINGERS* SO YOU CAN *TYPE* ON IT!

YOU *DON'T* TYPE ON IT! IT'S TOTALLY *VOICE-* CONTROLLED!

LIKE, *I* HAD AN IDEA FOR AN INVENTION!

I WAS WORKING ON *"FREEZE-DRIED WATER,"* BUT IT KEEPS *MELTING!*

REAH! ROO ROLD! BRRRR!

HELP! HELP!

DADDY!

YOU'RE *SAFE*, SIR! THERE'S *NOBODY* HERE!

PLEASE, MELISSA! PLEASE!

OH, NO, SIR, YOU'RE *MISTAKEN!* I'M VELMA AND SHE'S DAPHNE!

MELISSA IS MY *MOTHER'S* NAME, HE'S HEARING HER *VOICE* AGAIN!

OKAY, MR. WISENHEIMER, LET'S SEE YOU THROW YOUR VOICE *NOW!*

SHAGGY, *WHAT* ARE YOU DOING?

THE REASON MR. HUGHES IS HEARING VOICES IS BECAUSE *THIS* DUDE'S A *VEN-TRICKY-LIST!*

SHAGGY, IF HE WAS A *VENTRILOQUIST*, WE'D *ALL* HEAR THE VOICE!

HMM, LIKE, THAT *ALMOST* MAKES SENSE!

YOU *CAN'T* JUST MAKE *WILD ACCUSATIONS!* YOU HAVE TO COLLECT CLUES *BEFORE* YOU CAN SOLVE A MYSTERY!

WHY DON'T YOU GUYS DO WHAT YOU DO BEST? GO *ACT SCARED* AND FIND *SOMETHING TO EAT!*

LIKE, WE CAN TAKE A HINT. COME ON, SCOOBY!

WHO CARES ABOUT LOOKING FOR A DUMB OLD GHOST?

ROAST?

NOT TOAST-- GHOST!

MAYBE THE *GOOD* GOODIES ARE IN HERE... *ZOINKS...?!?* A *SECRET ENTRANCE??*

FOOSH

HELP! THE GHOST IS AFTER US!

WHERE DID YOU TWO COME FROM?

THEY CAME OUT OF THE SECRET TUNNELS THAT ARE BUILT ALL THROUGH THIS HOUSE!

TAKE YOUR FRIENDS AND LEAVE IMMEDIATELY, SCRUFFY!

THAT GHOST! AND SHE CALLED ME "SCRUFFY!"

YOU MEAN THIS GHOST THAT'S COMING FROM THIS MINIATURE HOLOGRAPHIC PROJECTOR THAT YOU KNOCKED OUT OF THE BOOKCASE?

HOW LONG HAVE YOU BEEN ABLE TO HEAR THE GHOST?

EVER SINCE SCOOBY STEPPED ON MY EAR!

STEPPED ON YOUR EAR? WAS YOUR HEAD ON THE FLOOR?

LIKE, NOT THAT I RECALL!

LET ME SEE YOUR EAR!

JUST AS I THOUGHT! A MINIATURE RECEIVER!

THERE'S ONE ON DAD'S EAR, TOO!

THEN I'M NOT HEARING THINGS!

OH, YOU'RE *HEARING* THINGS, ALL RIGHT!

BUT IT'S WHATEVER SOMEONE *WANTS* YOU TO HEAR!

AND HERE COMES THAT *SOMEONE* NOW!

LUKE, STOP PUSHING ME!

MOTHER, *I'M NOT* PUSHING *YOU*... *SOMEONE'S* PUSHING *ME!*

LUKE, *WHAT* IS THIS ALL ABOUT?

MELISSA, WHAT WERE YOU DOING DOWN IN THE CATACOMBS?

TRYING TO DRIVE *YOU* INSANE-- BY TRANSMITTING HER VOICE THROUGH THAT *EAR GADGET!*

I'VE BEEN TRYING TO GET YOU TO RETIRE AND LET *LUKE* TAKE OVER THE COMPANY FOR *YEARS*, YOU OLD *FOOL!*

AND IT WOULD HAVE WORKED THIS TIME, EVEN IF I HAD TO HAVE YOU DECLARED *INCOMPETENT!*

BUT, LIKE, I DON'T GET IT! WHY DID THEY JUST *COME OUT* WHEN THEIR PLAN WAS WORKING SO WELL?

WHEN WE MADE YOU LEAVE, WE SENT RALPH-- IN THE CHAMELEON SUIT-- AFTER YOU!

OVER A THOUSAND YEARS AGO, THE EMPEROR OF CHINA POSSESSED A MYSTERIOUS GLOWING GREEN STONE, FILLED WITH GREAT POWER, CALLED **THE DRAGON'S EYE.**

THE EMPEROR CUT THE STONE INTO SEVEN SMALLER, INTERLOCKING STONES, WHICH HE DISTRIBUTED AMONG HIS SONS. OVER TIME, THE STONES WERE SCATTERED AROUND THE WORLD.

NOW, SOME MYSTERIOUS VILLAIN IS STEALING THESE STONES. HE'S OUT-WITTED THE MYSTERY INC. GANG IN **PARIS, MOSCOW,** AND **ROME,** BUT WILL HE BEAT THEM IN...

DAMASCUS, SYRIA

YES, THE ITALIAN AUTHORITIES WARNED US ABOUT THE **TROUBLE** WE MIGHT EXPECT, AND ALSO INFORMED US OF YOUR OFFER TO AID US, BUT...

SCOOBY-DOO IN THE DRAGON'S EYE

PART 4: THE MASK IN Damascus

JOHN ROZUM
WRITER
JOE STATON
PENCILLER
HORACIO OTTOLINI
INKER
TOM ORZECHOWSKI
LETTERER
PAUL BECTON
COLORIST
DIGITAL CHAMELEON
SEPARATIONS
HARVEY RICHARDS
ASSISTANT EDITOR
JOAN HILTY
EDITOR

...I'M AFRAID YOU ARE *TOO LATE!*

THE STONE'S BEEN STOLEN?

"STONE"? MY DEAR BOY, CLEARLY YOU HAVE NOT SEEN PICTURES OF WHAT WE HAVE LOST-- OTHERWISE YOU WOULD NOT REFER TO IT AS A MERE **STONE!**

AND TO SAY IT WAS **"STOLEN,"** HMMPH, THAT IMPLIES MERE **BURGLARS,** BUT WHAT WE HAD HERE WAS--- WELL, LET ME TELL YOU...

THE "STONE," AS YOU CALL IT, WAS ACTUALLY PART OF A NECKLACE KNOWN AS 'THE DREAMING JEWEL.' IT'S NOT THE SORT OF ITEM WE WOULD NORMALLY DISPLAY HERE.

THIS IS A MUSEUM OF *ARCHAEOLOGY,* NOT *FINE ARTS,* AND THE NECKLACE WAS SET SOMETIME IN THE LAST FIVE HUNDRED YEARS-- FAR TOO RECENT FOR US!

"HOWEVER, IT WAS CLEARLY *PRICELESS*-- AND AS WE WERE AWARE THAT ONLY *SIX* OTHER PIECES LIKE IT WERE KNOWN TO EXIST, WE KEPT IT.

"WHEN THE AUTHORITIES IN ROME INFORMED US ABOUT THE OTHER THEFTS, WE QUICKLY DEACTIVATED ALL OF THE SECURITY DEVICES--

"--AND PREPARED TO HAVE THE DREAMING JEWEL REMOVED AND LOCKED IN A SECURE VAULT."

MRAOWWWR!

"PERHAPS IT WAS BAD TIMING, PERHAPS IT WOULD NOT HAVE MATTERED, BUT...

"...AT THAT MOMENT *ANWAT*--AN *UTUKKU,* OR DEMONIC MONSTER FROM OUR MYTHOLOGY, ENTERED THE HALL! HE OVER-POWERED THE GUARDS...

"...AND SEIZED THE NECKLACE-- *VANISHING* AS SUDDENLY AS HE APPEARED!"

THE MONSTER'S *GONE*?

AW, LIKE, *TOO BAD* WE MISSED HIM!

AW, *RARN!*

SNAP!

TO BE HONEST, WE'VE BEEN SO FOCUSED ON THE TROUBLE *OUTSIDE* THE MUSEUM--

--THAT WE WEREN'T REALLY PREPARED FOR ANYTHING TO GO WRONG *INSIDE!*

YES, WE HAD TO FIGHT THROUGH THAT TO GET INSIDE. WHAT'S IT ALL ABOUT, MR. an-NADIM?

UNFORTUNATELY, NOTHING NEW. MANY OF OUR RELICS COME FROM SITES CONSIDERED HOLY TO ISLAM, JUDAISM, AND CHRISTIANITY. WE ALSO SUPERVISE DIGS IN THOSE SITES.

SOME OF THE PROTESTERS OUTSIDE ARE UPSET THAT NON-ISLAMIC RELICS ARE DISPLAYED--THEY FEEL IT'S AS IF WE WERE HONORING *INFIDEL GODS.*

OTHERS THINK THAT TAKING *ANY* RELICS FROM A HOLY SITE SHOULDN'T BE DONE AT ALL.

BUT AS DIRECTOR OF THIS MUSEUM, PRESERVATION OF THESE ARTIFACTS IS THE ONLY CONCERN I HAVE. WE CAN'T LEARN FROM ANYTHING THAT REMAINS BURIED IN THE GROUND.

ROME, ITALY.

THE OFFICES OF INTERPOL, THE INTERNATIONAL POLICE.

I SURE HOPE THE BOYS ARE HAVING BETTER LUCK THAN WE ARE.

I WISH I COULD BE OF MORE HELP, BUT I NEVER GOT A GOOD LOOK AT YOUR MYSTERY MAN.

KEEPING ME COMPANY IS HELPING ME PLENTY, VELMA. OTHERWISE, I'D FEEL LIKE I MADE A TERRIBLE MISTAKE!

YOU NEED A BREAK? WE COULD GO GRAB DINNER. WITHOUT SHAGGY AND SCOOBY HERE, WE'D EVEN GET TO EAT SOME OF IT!

NO, NOT YET. THIS IS THE LAST BOOK. IF HE'S NOT IN HERE, HE'S NOT ANYWHERE. HE CERTAINLY WASN'T IN THEIR COMPUTER FILES.

NOT FINDING HIM IN INTERPOL RECORDS ONLY MEANS THAT YOUR MYSTERY MAN WAS NEVER CONVICTED OF A CRIME. SO, EVEN IF HE'S NOT IN THAT BOOK, HE'S STILL SOMEWHERE...

...AND WE'LL FIND HIM!

WE HAVE TO. HE'S THE ONLY LEAD WE'VE GOT.

HE WAS THE ONLY LEAD WE HAD. WHEN YOU'RE FINISHED, LET ME SHOW YOU SOMETHING I'VE BEEN WORKING ON!

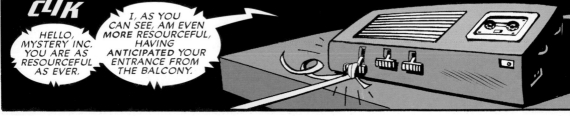

SNIFF RELLS RUNNY...

ROMB!

A BOMB?!

WHERE?!

REAH! ROMB!

CLIK

KABOOM!

PONK